Rabbit Helps Out

Tales from Whispery Wood

Make friends with the animals of Whispery Wood!

Be sure to read:

Mole's Useful Day

Flying Friends

Owl's Big Mistake

... and lots, lots more!

Rabbit Helps Out

Julia Jarman
illustrated by Guy Parker-Rees

SCHOLASTIC

To Sam and Theo – J.J.

Scholastic Children's Books,
Commonwealth House, 1-19 New Oxford Street,
London, WC1A 1NU, UK
a division of Scholastic Ltd
London ~ New York ~ Toronto ~ Sydney ~ Auckland
Mexico City ~ New Delhi ~ Hong Kong

First published by Scholastic Ltd, 2003

ISBN 0 439 97811 4

Printed and bound in Singapore

10 9 8 7 6 5 4 3 2 1

Chapter One

It was a spring morning in Whispery Wood.
Owl and Bat were asleep in the old oak tree.
They had been hard at work all night,
carrying litter to litter bins.

All the other animals were busy spring cleaning too – all except Rabbit, who couldn't get out of his burrow.

Suddenly Squirrel dashed by.

"Good morning, lazy lump!" he shouted,
heading for his drey with a bundle of clean
grass.

"Oh Squirrel, I'm not lazy," said Rabbit.
"I can't get out. I'm
waiting for Badger to
lift this branch out of
the way. Bat told
him about it
last night."

"Only joking," laughed Squirrel, "I'm sure you'll be able to help later. Enjoy the rest while you can, Rabbit!"

But Rabbit didn't enjoy the rest. He started to worry. "Am I really lazy?"

He was still worrying when Mole popped up. "Hello, Rabbit! Have you heard this joke?"

Mole came to see Rabbit every morning, and she always told him a joke. It was good fun. Rabbit always laughed when Mole told him the answer. And he never said, "I've heard that one before," even though he usually had.

"Mole," said Rabbit anxiously,
"do you think I'm lazy?"

But Mole didn't hear Rabbit. She was
thinking about her joke.

"Listen to this one," she said. "What
makes a tree noisy?"

"I don't know," said Rabbit. "What does make a tree noisy?"

Mole barked like a dog.

"Bark! Bark! The bark. Get it?"

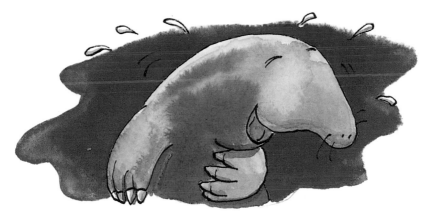

She waited for Rabbit to laugh, but Rabbit didn't. "Oh dear. What's wrong with you today?" said Mole.

"I want to help with the spring clean," said Rabbit, "but I can't get out."

"Course you can, you lazy lump,"
laughed Mole. "You can dig another exit,
can't you? I'd stay to help but I've still got
tunnels to clean."

And Mole dashed off, not realizing she'd
hurt Rabbit's feelings.

"Lazy lump," Rabbit said to himself,
as he dug another exit. "Mole called me
a lazy lump, and so did Squirrel. Why
didn't I think of digging my way out?
Am I lazy?"

He hopped out of his new exit and looked
all around. Whispery Wood was clean and
tidy. The other animals had been very
busy. Hedgehog was picking up the last bit
of litter on his spikes.

"Oh Hedgehog, can I help?" asked Rabbit.

"Thanks Rabbit, but I've finished now," said Hedgehog.

There was nothing left to do. Rabbit felt sad and useless.

Chapter Two

In the afternoon Squirrel came to see
Rabbit. "I'm just off to Hazel Copse to fetch
some nuts from my store," he said. "Could
you keep an ear open for Little Squirrel,
please? He's having a nap. If he wakes up,
tell him I won't be long, will you?"

"Of course I will," said Rabbit eagerly. "I'll keep two ears open, and I'll sing him a song and I'll play games with him. I want to help, I really do."

Rabbit sat listening, longing for Little Squirrel to wake up, but he was still asleep when his dad got back.

"Thank you, Rabbit," said Squirrel. "That was a big help."

"Was it?" said Rabbit. "Was it really? I was trying not to be a l-lazy l-lump."

"Oh Rabbit, I didn't mean it," said Squirrel, scampering up the tree to Little Squirrel. "You're not lazy. Please forget what I said!"

But Rabbit
couldn't forget.
Lazy lump.
He couldn't get
the words out
of his head.

"What's the matter?" said Owl, when he
woke up and saw Rabbit's droopy ears.

"Oh Owl, you and Bat and all the other
animals have been busy spring cleaning,
and I've done nothing, nothing at all. I've
been a lazy rabbit."

"Rabbit," said Owl. "You know that's not true. Squirrel just told me you helped him a lot this afternoon. Now do stop worrying."

"Look," said Owl, "here's Badger, come to move the fallen branch. I'd better go because he doesn't like too much company, but I'll be back later with Bat."

Badger came ambling out of the darkness.
He was a shy creature who sounded much
grumpier than he was.

"Oh Badger, thank you for coming," said
Rabbit.

"Glad to help. No trouble," said Badger,
lifting the branch out of the way.

But then he saw Rabbit's new exit.
"What's that?" he asked.

"Needn't have come," he said when
Rabbit explained. Poor Rabbit!
He threw up his paws
in dismay.

"Oh Badger. I'm so sorry. So sorry.
I shouldn't have bothered you. I really
shouldn't. Oh, oh, oh!"
He buried his head
in his paws.

When Bat and Owl got back, Rabbit had disappeared into his burrow and he wouldn't come out.

"We've got to do something," squeaked Bat. "Quickly. We've got to prove to Rabbit that he's not lazy and cheer him up."

Chapter Three

Luckily Owl had a good idea. He called a
meeting to tell everyone about it.

"We're going to have a race," he said.

"What sort of race?" asked Hedgehog.

"A hop, skip and jump race – from the old oak tree to the big chestnut tree."

"Oh good," said Squirrel, "I might win that."

"I, er ... hope you won't," said Owl. "I'd really like Rabbit to win. As you can see, he isn't here. He's in his burrow feeling very down. We're having the race to cheer him up."

"I see," said Squirrel. "Good idea. I didn't mean to, but I hurt his feelings."

"So did I," said Mole.

"But he's ever so good at hop, skip and jump," said Hedgehog. "He'll win and that will cheer him up!"

"And that will prove he's not lazy!" said Mole. "You can't win races if you're lazy. You have to try really hard."

"Exactly," said Owl.

All the animals wanted to help.

"I'll be a judge and hold the finishing line," said Squirrel.

"I'll hold the other end," said Bat.

"I'll race, but I'm not good at hop, skip and jump," said Mole.

"Nor am I," said Hedgehog, "but I'll race too. Rabbit's sure to win."

"If we can persuade him to take part,"
said Owl. "I'll go and talk to him first thing
tomorrow morning."

Rabbit was playing conkers with Little Squirrel when Owl called.

Little Squirrel's conker rolled out of the burrow. Rabbit chased after it.

"You're a kind, hard-working animal, Rabbit," said Owl.

"Oh, I'm just playing, really," said Rabbit. "It's not work."

Owl sighed and shook his head. It was going to be hard work convincing Rabbit he wasn't lazy.

He told Rabbit about the race. "It's this evening," he said. "And we'd all like you to take part. It wouldn't be much fun without you."

Rabbit looked worried. "I'm not sure," he said.

"Why ever not?" asked Owl. "You're brilliant at hop, skip and jump!"

"It's Little Squirrel," said
Rabbit. "Won't he be asleep?
And won't Squirrel be at the race?
I've told him that I'll always
squirrel-sit when he goes out.
I do so want to be helpful."

"I know you do," said Owl. "We all do, but Robin can squirrel-sit tonight. We need you to make it an exciting race. You will come, won't you, Rabbit?"

"Okay. As long as Squirrel doesn't mind," said Rabbit.

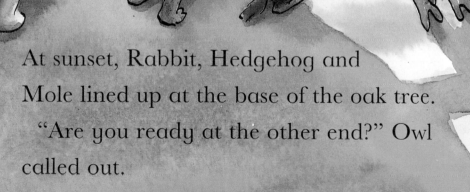

Chapter Four

At sunset, Rabbit, Hedgehog and
Mole lined up at the base of the oak tree.

"Are you ready at the other end?" Owl
called out.

"Yes we are!" Squirrel and Bat called back.

"Right!" Owl held up his wing. "Ready! Stead—"

"Wait!" cried a croaky voice – and there was Frog, jumping on to the starting line beside Mole. "Just heard about the race," he croaked. "Can I join in?"

"Oh no," muttered Mole. "Frog's ace at hopping and jumping!"

"Not bad at skipping either," said Hedgehog.

Owl said, "You are rather late, Frog." Frog looked glum.

"Do let him race," said Rabbit. "He's fast. You said you wanted it to be exciting."

Hedgehog said, "But Frog might—"

"Shush," said Mole, giving him a nudge.

"Please Owl," said Rabbit. "It wouldn't be fair not to include Frog."

"You are right of course, Rabbit," said Owl. "Okay Frog, line up."

Reluctantly Owl raised his wing again.
"Ready! Steady! Go!"

Frog shot into the lead.

"Oh no," squeaked Bat.

"Don't worry," said Squirrel, "Rabbit's coming up fast. He's trying really hard. Come on! Come on, Rabbit!" he couldn't help cheering.

By the time they reached the hawthorn
bush Frog and Rabbit were neck and neck.
Hedgehog and Mole were way behind.
And then Rabbit moved into the lead!
"Come on, you can do it!" urged Squirrel.
"Go for it!" squeaked Bat.

Then it went quiet, so quiet all you could hear was the racers' feet pounding towards the finishing line. Frog caught up. It was neck and neck again. Then Rabbit moved into the lead again. He was bounding ahead. It looked as if he was going to win...

...when suddenly he stopped and Frog overtook him!

"I won! I won!" croaked Frog as he hopped over the line.

"What are you doing, Rabbit?" yelled Mole and Hedgehog as Rabbit ran past them in the opposite direction.

Bat whizzed overhead squeaking, "I think I know what he's doing, I'll go and see!"

Chapter Five

Bat arrived at the oak tree at the same time as Rabbit, and there was Little Squirrel sobbing.

Rabbit put a paw round him. "What's the matter, Little Squirrel?"

"I w-woke up and my d-dad wasn't there, s-so I went to find you and y-you weren't there!"

"I was here," said Robin. "But he only wanted you."

"And here I am," said Rabbit. "I came as soon as I heard you crying."

"Please don't g-go again," sniffed Little Squirrel.

"I won't," said Rabbit as the other animals arrived. "I'll always be here for you, under the oak tree."

"Exactly," said Owl. "That's what you're exceedingly good at, Rabbit. Being here for all of us. You're always here when I want someone to talk to."

"And when I want someone to tell jokes to," said Mole.

"And when I want someone to watch my aerobatics," said Bat.

"So let's hear no more about you being lazy," said Owl. "When Little Squirrel needed you, you rushed to his side. Lazy animals don't rush."

46

"Abso-tootly," squeaked Bat. "Listen, I've made up a rhyme about you."

You're a rabbit with a habit
Of listening really well.
At caring for others
You really do excel.
So three big cheers
For the listening habit
Of our very good friend
The Always There Rabbit!

"Abso-hootly!" hooted Owl.

"Abso-rootly!" shouted Mole.

All the animals cheered loudly and
Rabbit looked very, very happy.